I Get Loud

First published in Great Britain in 2021 by Canongate Books Ltd,
14 High Street, Edinburgh EH1 1TE

canongate.co.uk

1

British Library Cataloguing-in-Publication Data
A catalogue record for this book is available on
request from the British Library

ISBN 978 1 78689 777 0

Printed and bound in China by C&C (Offset)

I Get Loud

David Ouimet

CANONGATE

Sometimes, I get loud.

When I am swept
into the light of life
I feel my heart lift.

So I get loud.

You hear my song

and turn towards me.

I see you, you see me.

You are small and brave;
with you, I feel free and loud.

We speak

and sing;

we laugh

and stutter.

Have you ever screamed
underwater as loud as you could?

Don't
you
know
that we
are louder

together?

Sometimes

the wind bre_{ak} s

what was bound.

We know how colours can fade

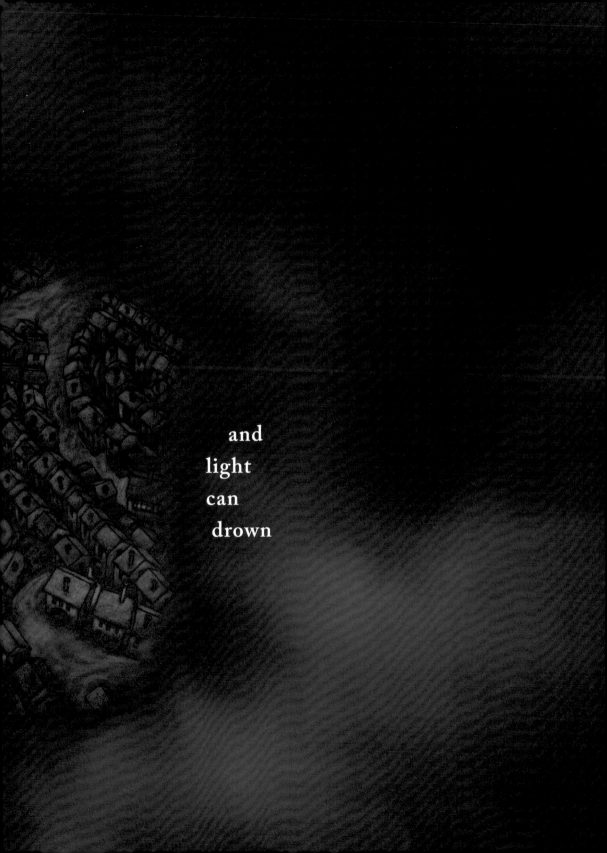

and
light
can
drown

when our roots are pulled
from our broken ground.

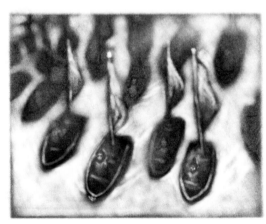

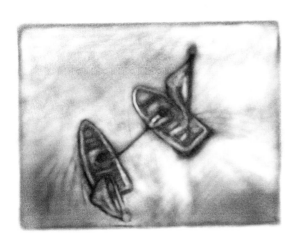

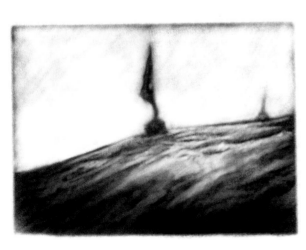

We were

louder

together.

Alone,

I

go

quiet.

Sometimes, the wind
binds what was broken.

In the
jumble
of voices
I hear

the only one
I know.

I shout,
you gasp;
I mew,
you roar.

Our songs will rise;

our voices will surge.

Because we are louder

together.

We are bound by endless stories.

Our sounds
are stairs, singing.

Our worlds are
windows, laughing.

Our hearts are our home shimmering;

with you
I
get
loud.